THIS CANDLEWICK BOOK BELONGS TO:

_____

_____

_____

_____

AMY HEST and Jill Barton collaborated on all of the Baby Duck books. "When I saw Jill's illustrations," Amy recalls after seeing the first book, "I loved them so much I sat down and wrote two more stories about Baby Duck." There are now four books about this plucky duck heroine and her family. Amy Hest is the author of many other books for children, including the middle-grade novels about another memorable heroine: *Love You, Soldier; The Private Notebook of Katie Roberts, Age 11;* and *The Great Green Notebook of Katie Roberts.*

JILL BARTON drew on her memories of her own grandfather to illustrate the Baby Duck books. "He always made the time to listen," she recalls. Jill Barton is the illustrator of many picture books, including *What Baby Wants* and *Rattletrap Car* by Phyllis Root and *The Pig in the Pond* and *The Happy Hedgehog Band* by Martin Waddell.

After that, Baby Duck pulled Hot Stuff all around the yard. She sang a little song.

"Brand-new babies are a pain,
Fuss, fuss, fuss, fuss, fuss.
Maybe you can stay two days,
But Baby Duck is boss!"

"Look at me!" Baby rolled over.

Hot Stuff looked.

She burbled.

"Now I will read you a story."
Baby turned pages
in her book.

Hot Stuff gurgled. She giggled and
burbled and babbled.

"No crying," Baby said. "I'm the boss."

Hot Stuff did not cry.

"Look at me!"

Baby hopped on one foot.

Hot Stuff looked.

She gurgled.

After lunch Baby put Hot Stuff
in her wagon.

And of course the lemonade.

The sandwiches were a big hit.

Baby Duck and Grampa made sandwiches
with jam. Baby got the bread. Grampa
got some jam.

"Not that jam," Baby said. "*That* one."

"You're the boss, Baby Duck," Grampa said.

"Yes," Baby said. "I am!"

"Brand-new babies are bad helpers,"
Baby said.

"Oh, yes," Grampa said. "Brand-new babies
don't do much. They don't know how."

Baby Duck and Grampa made lemonade.

Grampa squeezed lemons.

Baby poured sugar.

"You are a good helper," Grampa said.

Grampa was waiting at the kitchen door.

He looked in the carriage.

"Welcome," he said.

Then he kissed Baby's cheeks.

"Bad day?" he asked.

"Yes," Baby said.

"Some people make
a great big fuss when
there's a brand-new baby
in the house," Grampa said.

"Yes," Baby said.

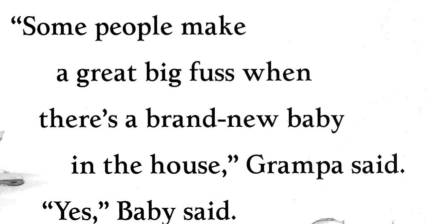

"I am making lunch," Grampa
said. "Want to help?"

"Yes," Baby said.

"Time to show Grampa your brand-new baby sister!" called Mr. and Mrs. Duck.

Baby Duck stomped along. She dragged her feet and mumbled.

"That bad baby is in my carriage,
Wearing my nice coat.
I hope she goes away today
And stays away forever."

Mr. Duck tucked
Hot Stuff into
Baby's old
carriage.

They did not hear her read.

Baby Duck turned
pages in her book.
"I can read,"
she said.

Mrs. Duck put Hot Stuff into Baby's old coat.

Baby rolled over.

"Look at me!"

Mr. Duck tickled Hot Stuff on her
fat little feet. He forgot to look.

Baby got up and hopped on
one foot. "Look at me!"

Mrs. Duck kissed Hot Stuff on her
fat little beak. She forgot to look.

Baby Duck sat by herself. She sang a little song.

"Send that no-good Hot Stuff back,
No one wants her here.
Her beak is fat, her feet are fat,
And I'm the only baby."

"Are you singing to your baby sister?"
called Mr. Duck. "What a fine sister you are!"
Baby stopped singing.

Baby Duck was having a bad day.
There was a brand-new baby in the house,
and everyone was making a great big fuss
for no good reason.

"What a fine little face," cooed Mrs. Duck.

"Don't you love her little beak?"

"No," Baby said.

"What fine little feet," trilled Mr. Duck.

"Isn't she hot stuff?"

"No," Baby said.

You're the Boss,
Baby Duck!

Amy Hest

illustrated by **Jill Barton**

CANDLEWICK PRESS
CAMBRIDGE, MASSACHUSETTS

For the real boss,
Sam Hest
A. H.

For Sophie
and the new baby
J. B.

Text copyright © 1997 by Amy Hest
Illustrations copyright © 1997 by Jill Barton

First U.S. paperback edition 2001

The Library of Congress has cataloged the hardcover edition as follows:

Hest, Amy.
You're the boss, Baby Duck / Amy Hest ; illustrated by
Jill Barton. — 1st U.S. ed.
Summary: When her parents make such a fuss over their new baby, Baby Duck
feels neglected, until Grampa helps her to realize that she is still important.
ISBN 1-56402-667-1 (hardcover)
[1. Ducks—Fiction. 2. Babies—Fiction. 3. Grandfathers—Fiction.]
I. Barton, Jill, ill. II. Title.
PZ7.H4375Yo   1997
[E]—dc21   96-46640

ISBN 0-7636-0801-7 (paperback)

2 4 6 8 10 9 7 5 3 1

Printed in Hong Kong

This book was typeset in Opti Lucius Ad Bold.
The illustrations were done in pencil and watercolor.

Candlewick Press
2067 Massachusetts Avenue
Cambridge, Massachusetts 02140

visit us at www.candlewick.com